Haka Boy
a rugby league story

-

Tom Palmer

-

Illustrated by James Innerdale

-

Harry watched Mr Donaldson hand out pieces of paper to the class.

The teacher did not say what the pieces of paper were for, but Harry still took one and said thank you.

On his piece of paper he read the words 'New Zealand.'

Harry knew that New Zealand was a group of islands in the Pacific. He had learned about every country in the world, looking at an Atlas in the library. But that was all he knew about New Zealand.

Soon Mr Donaldson began to speak.
'Each of you has been handed the name of
a country,' he explained. 'All of the countries
are playing in the Rugby League World Cup
this autumn. Your homework is to find out
about your country.'

'Do we have to write an essay?' one of the other children asked.

'Good question,' Mr Donaldson answered. 'No. Some of you will be asked to talk about your country in assembly on Monday.'

'Yessss!' I've got England,' Molly Hogg, sitting next to Harry, said.

Harry laughed with everyone else in the classroom, but he was glad that he didn't have England. He was excited to have a country he knew little about. Now he would be able to look at books in the library and at interesting websites on the internet. He loved projects like this.

'Hello Harry,' Mrs Dahl, the librarian, said, as Harry walked into the brightly lit library that was near his house.

'Hi Mrs Dahl.'

'What are you looking for today?'

'Books on New Zealand, please?'

'New Zealand? Okay...'

Mrs Dahl led Harry to the far end of the library. She was not surprised that Harry wanted to know about New Zealand. He was always asking about interesting things.

And it was her job to find them for him. She loved filling children's minds with stories and dreams.

The library was buzzing with people. Some children were doing colouring at a table in the corner. But Harry sat looking through the book that Mrs Dahl had found. It included a whole chapter about New Zealand.

He became so interested in these islands on the other side of the world that he kept reading for nearly an hour.

He found out that New Zealand was made up of nearly 100 islands.

That it is so far away from other countries it has animals and birds that don't exist anywhere else.

And that its native people, the Maoris, had lived in New Zealand for hundreds of years before the Europeans arrived.

All the time he was discovering about New Zealand, Harry knew he felt a little funny. Like he was going down with a cold. Or about to be sick.

So, feeling tired, he stopped to wonder what was wrong.

And immediately he knew.

He had been so excited about finding out about a new country, he had forgotten what Mr Donaldson had told them.

That some of them would have to talk about it in assembly.

No.

Not that.

Anything but that.

Harry now felt really nervous.

Nervous that he could be asked to speak in assembly.

He felt sick.

Properly sick.

And dizzy.

He felt bad bad bad.

That night, when his mum had switched off his bedroom light, Harry stared into the darkness. A darkness that seemed to stretch on forever, not just to the walls of his small bedroom.

Harry was remembering the last time he had spoken in front of assembly. It had been during a Christmas play. Harry had been a wise man. But when it came to saying his line, he had started to cry, then had run out of the school hall.

Harry had been five then. He had avoided talking to large groups of people ever since, even in class.

And now he was worried. Because he knew he would not be able to sleep. He had found out ten really interesting facts about New Zealand, but he didn't think he would be able to tell them to anyone in the morning.

At five in the morning, Harry gave up trying to go to sleep and went down to the kitchen. He made himself a bowl of cereal and started to look at the family iPad. He was allowed to do this if he woke up early. Now that he was nine.

He used the search techniques that Mrs Dahl had taught him to find things on the internet, typing "watch New Zealand playing rugby league".

He quickly found a video. But, once it had started, Harry could not believe what he was looking at. The whole New Zealand team was standing facing their opponents doing a sort of war dance.

They thrust their arms out.

They stamped their feet.

They stuck their tongues out.

It was crazy.

It was mad.

But Harry loved it.

The war dance was called the haka. Harry found out that there were several hakas performed by nations like Tonga, who were also taking part in the Rugby League World Cup.

Knowing that the rest of the world was asleep, Harry stood up and tried to copy the New Zealand players.

To do what they were doing.
To shout what they were shouting.
And it felt great.

Harry must have done the haka twenty times before he saw his dad standing at the foot of the stairs, rubbing his eyes.

'Harry? What are you doing?'

Harry stopped doing the haka and shut the iPad.

'Nothing,' he said, expecting to be told off for waking his parents.

'Nothing?' Dad grinned. 'Well, whatever that nothing was, it was amazing. I loved it. Now... go back to bed!'

The sun was streaming into the school hall as 220 children gathered and sat, little ones at the front, the bigger ones on the benches at the back.

'We have an important guest today,' the head teacher, Mrs Morpurgo announced. 'In a few minutes one of the players from the Rugby League World Cup is visiting us.'

A chatter spread quickly through the hall. But Mrs Morpurgo raised her hand and soon 220 children had raised their hands too. All was quiet now.

'But first, Mr Donaldson's class is going to make three presentations,' Mrs Morpurgo said. 'Who's first, Mr Donaldson?'

Harry swallowed. *Please not me. Please not me.* He said it over and over in his head.

'Rebecca Page can go first,' Mr Donaldson smiled. 'She'll be talking about Italy.'

Harry breathed out.

One down: two to go. Maybe he would not have to speak.

After Rebecca Page spoke about pizza and Pisa in Italy, Simon Mawson stood to talk about Fiji. Harry was amazed how confident Simon seemed. He didn't look nervous at all.

Why am I so rubbish? he said to himself. *Why can't I just go up there and talk, like everyone else?*

'Right, Mr Donaldson said when Simon had finished. 'One left. Let's have...'

But Mr Donaldson stopped speaking when a giant man appeared in the doorway of the assembly hall with the school secretary.

'This is Puti Halifax, the rugby star,' the school secretary announced. 'He's from New Zealand.'

The whole hall began to clap and cheer. There was a huge excitement now.

But Harry did not feel excitement. He knew what was going to happen next. It was obvious.

When the clapping died down, Mr Donaldson glanced around the hall.

Harry looked down, hoping the teacher would not see him.

But Mr Donaldson had the eyes of a hawk. Harry saw Mr Donaldson's shoes before he heard his voice.

'There you are, Harry,' his teacher said. 'I'd like you to tell everyone about New Zealand. I know you've worked really hard on this. Mrs Dahl in the library told me. Would you like to come to the front?'

Harry slowly got to his feet.

He walked through the year fours, then the year threes.

He reached the front of the school hall. Then he turned round, 220 children and at least ten teachers staring back at him.

And so was Puti Halifax. The New Zealand rugby league star.

Puti Halifax winked at Harry.

He knows, Harry thought. *He knows I am too scared to speak.*

Harry knew that he was standing at the front saying nothing.

The bad news was that his mind was going round and round on itself, meaning that everything he had planned to say about New Zealand was gone.

The good news was that he had not run out of the hall crying. Yet.

It wasn't until he heard other children begin to laugh that he knew he couldn't just stand there and do nothing.

Next he heard a voice he knew well. Molly Hogg's voice.

'Harry's forgotten what to say' she mocked. 'Loser.'

'Be quiet Molly,' a teacher's voice called out.

Silence again.

Harry looked at the far end of the hall. If Puti Halifax had not been standing there, maybe he could just run through the door. He wasn't sure where he would run.

Just away. Away from here. Away from this.

But the doorway was blocked by this massive man.

And Molly Hogg's words had struck home.

She was right. He had forgotten what to say. He was a loser.

'Harry?'

It was Mr Donaldson's voice.

'Harry? Are you ready to start?'

Harry looked at his teacher. His body felt like jelly.

'Why don't you start with the first thing you remember?' Mr Donaldson suggested, kindly.

But Harry could not remember the *first* thing he had meant to say. Nor the *second*. Nor the *third*. There was nothing in his head. Nothing at all. It was still empty.

Now the laughter began again. A few children around the hall finding it funny that Harry had forgotten what to say.

And all the teachers' hushing could do nothing to stop it.

Harry looked across the school hall in despair. Right into the eyes of Puti Halifax The haka was the first thing that came into his mind, looking at the rugby star. The faces of the New Zealand players as they performed the haka.

The moves.

The chants.

The rhythms.

And the feeling that Harry had had that morning doing the haka in the kitchen came back to him.

Add so he began.

Harry put his feet wide apart, then stamped his left foot down hard.

He shouted.

He thrust his arms in front of his chest and stared at all the children. Some were laughing, others were chattering, asking each other what Harry was doing.

Then he stuck his tongue out as far as it would go.

Harry thrust out his leg.

Shouted again.

Crouched.

Punched the ground.

Beat his chest.

Launched himself into the haka, making it as loud and violent as he could.

And now the audience was silent. Utterly silent. Staring at him. Eyes huge. Mouths open.

At the back of the hall Puti Halifax was nodding. So Harry went on. Louder. Harder. Faster. Repeating the moves he had seen the New Zealand team doing on the internet that morning.

And it felt good.

It felt so good.

Harry had silenced the school hall.

And the hall was *so* silent that, after he had stopped his war dance, Harry could hear the school clock second hand ticking ten times. Add then the hall exploded with cheers and shouts and clapping, 220 faces grinning up at him.

Harry closed his eyes and breathed out.
He had got through his presentation.
He had done it.

Harry looked into Puti Halifax's eyes and smiled.

TRY READING

Get stuck into your local Library!

Public Libraries Supporting
Rugby League World Cup 2013
www.RLWC2013.com

Supported using public funding by
**ARTS COUNCIL
ENGLAND**

THIS BOOK WAS COMMISSIONED AS PART OF TRY READING, A MAJOR PROJECT THAT CELEBRATES AND PROMOTES THE SPORTING EVENT OF THE YEAR - RUGBY LEAGUE WORLD CUP 2013.

At the same time it encourages more people to read more and to have a go at writing and drama. The project is funded with an award from the National Lottery supported Grants for the arts libraries fund by Arts Council England.

Try Reading is a partnership between the North West, Yorkshire and Humber regions of the Society of Chief Librarians. There are 30 library services working together to provide a wide range of events and opportunities for people to engage with reading and writing through the website.

Public libraries are delighted to be supporting RLWC2013. For details of the tournament fixtures visit www.rlwc2013.com

For more information about Try Reading and the opportunity to submit your own writing and reading experiences visit the Try Reading website.

Schools and libraries can download the text of Haka Boy and find resources for activities to go with the book on the website.

The moral right of the author has been asserted
First published by Scratching Shed Publishing Ltd in 2013
Registered in England & Wales No. 6588772.
Registered office: 47 Street Lane, Leeds, West Yorkshire. LS8 1AP
www.scratchingshedpublishing.co.uk

ISBN 9780957559370